Little Goblins Ten

By **Pamela Jane**

Illustrated by **Jane Manning**

HARPER

An Imprint of HarperCollinsPublishers

Over in the forest

Where the trees hide the sun

Lived a big mommy monster

And her little monster one.

"Scare!" said the mommy;
"I scare," said the one.
So he scared and he scampered
Where the trees hide the sun.

Over in the forest
        Where spooks shout, "Boo!"
Lived a pale daddy ghost
        And his little ghosties two.

"Haunt!" cried the daddy;
  "We haunt," cried the two.
So they hid and they haunted
  Where spooks shout, "Boo!"

Over in the forest
    Near a gnarled oak tree
Lived an old mother zombie
    And her little zombies three.

"Stare!" said the mommy;
    "We stare," said the three.
So they stared all together
    Near the gnarled oak tree.

Over in the forest
Where the fierce winds roar
Lived a gray father werewolf
And his little wolvies four.

"Howl!" said the father;
"We howl," said the four.
So they howled and they growled
Where the fierce winds roar.

Over in the forest
    Where the shadows come alive
Lived an old mother mummy
    And her little mummies five.

"Moan!" said the mother;
"We moan," said the five.
So they moaned and they groaned
Where the shadows come alive.

Over in the forest
    In a hovel made of sticks
Lived an old mother witch
    And her little witches six.

"Cackle!" screeched the mother;
    "We cackle," screeched the six.
So they crowed and they cackled
    In the hovel made of sticks.

Over in the forest
In a mossy green heaven
Lived a scaly father dragon
And his little dragons seven.

"Breathe!" said the father;
  "We breathe," said the seven.
So they breathed flames of fire
  In the mossy green heaven.

Over in the forest
  By the graveyard gate
Lived a bony father skeleton
  And his little skellies eight.

"Rattle!" said the father;
  "We rattle," said the eight.
So they rattled and they ran
  By the graveyard gate.

Over in the forest
        Near a tall dark pine
Lived a furry mother bat
        And her little batties nine.

"Swoop!" cried the mother;
        "We swoop," cried the nine.
So they swooped in the shadows
        Near the tall dark pine.

Over in the forest
In a deep green glen
Lived an old father goblin
And his little goblins ten.

"Leap!" said the father;
  "We leap," said the ten.
So they laughed and they leaped
  In the deep green glen.

Over in the forest
    Where the trees hide the sun
The big mommy called
    To her little monster one.

"Trick or treat?" asked the mommy;
"Treat!" cried the one.
So they skipped off together
For some Halloween fun!

To my mother and father, who read to me
before I understood the words
—P.J.

To Mike and Judy, with love
—J.M.

Little Goblins Ten
Text copyright © 2011 by Pamela Jane
Illustrations copyright © 2011 by Jane Manning
All rights reserved. Manufactured in China.
No part of this book may be used or reproduced in any manner whatsoever without written permission except in the case of brief quotations
embodied in critical articles and reviews. For information address HarperCollins Children's Books, a division of HarperCollins Publishers,
10 East 53rd Street, New York, NY 10022.
www.harpercollinschildrens.com

Library of Congress Cataloging-in-Publication Data
Jane, Pamela.
   Little goblins ten / by Pamela Jane ; illustrated by Jane Manning. — 1st ed.
     p. cm.
   Summary: Ghouls, goblins, ghosts, witches, and other scary creatures cavort in the forest on Halloween, introducing the
numbers one through ten.
   ISBN 978-0-06-176798-2 (trade bdg.) — ISBN 978-0-06-176800-2 (lib. bdg.)
   [1. Stories in rhyme. 2. Halloween—Fiction. 3. Monsters—Fiction. 4. Counting.] I. Manning, Jane, ill. II. Title.
PZ8.3.J158Li 2011   2010010169
[E]—dc22   CIP
                                                                                                                                         AC

Typography by Jennifer Rozbruch
11 12 13 14 15   SCP   10 9 8 7 6 5 4 3 2 1
❖
First Edition